SPOTLIGHT ON THE AMERICAN INDIANS OF CALIFORNIA

THE MOHAVE

ANDREA PALMER

PowerKiDS press.

New York

Published in 2018 by The Rosen Publishing Group, Inc.
29 East 21st Street, New York, NY 10010

Editor: Melissa Raé Shofner
Book Design: Michael Flynn
Interior Layout: Rachel Rising

Photo Credits: Cover Werner Forman/Universal Images Group/Getty Images; p. 4 You Touch Pix of EuToch/Shutterstock.com; p. 5 https://en.wikipedia.org/wiki/File:Mosa,_Mohave_girl,_by_Edward_S._Curtis,_1903.jpg; p. 7 https://commons.wikimedia.org/wiki/File:Two_Mojave_Indians_girls_standing_in_front_of_a_small_dwelling_with_a_thatched_roof,_1900_(CHS-1241).jpg; p. 9 NaturesMomentsuk/Shutterstock.com; pp. 11, 19 Courtesy of the USC Digital Library; p. 13 https://commons.wikimedia.org/wiki/File:Doll,_Mohave,_acquired_in_1912_-_Native_American_collection_-_Peabody_Museum,_Harvard_University_-_DSC05514.JPG; p. 15 Buyenlarge/Archive Photos/Getty Images; pp. 17, 21, 25 Courtesy of the Library of Congress; pp. 18, 26 Courtesy of the New York Public Library Digtial Collections; p. 23 Science & Society Picture Library/SSPL/Getty Images; p. 27 Marzolino/Shutterstock.com; p. 29 https://commons.wikimedia.org/wiki/File:Parker,_Arizona._Henry_Welsh,_Mojave_Indian_and_chairman_of_the_tribal_council_of_the_Colorado_Rive_._._._-_NARA_-_536247.jpg.

Library of Congress Cataloging-in-Publication Data

Names: Palmer, Andrea, author.
Title: The Mohave / Andrea Palmer.
Description: New York : PowerKids Press, [2018] | Series: Spotlight on the American Indians of California | Includes index.
Identifiers: LCCN 2017025480| ISBN 9781538324738 (library bound) | ISBN 9781538324769 (pbk.) | ISBN 9781538324776 (6 pack)
Subjects: LCSH: Mohave Indians--Juvenile literature.
Classification: LCC E99.M77 P34 2018 | DDC 979.1004/975722--dc23
LC record available at https://lccn.loc.gov/2017025480

Manufactured in the United States of America

CPSIA Compliance Information: Batch #BW18PK For further information contact Rosen Publishing, New York, New York at 1-800-237-9932.

CONTENTS

CHAPTER ONE

MEET THE MOHAVE

Today, the Mohave Indians live in California and in parts of Arizona and Nevada. Their name—originally spelled "Mojave"—comes from the word *hamakhava*. *Hamakhava* is the Mohave name for a group of three mountains located near the modern town of Needles, California. When Spanish explorers heard this word, they thought it sounded like "Mojave" (moh-HAH-vay). Anglo Americans changed the spelling to "Mohave" to fit with English pronunciation rules.

The Mohave Indians have lived near the Colorado River for thousands of years. They call themselves the Pipa Aha Macav, which means "people who live along the water."

Scholars are still studying the history of the Mohave people. Most scholars think the Mohave moved to the Colorado River area thousands of years ago with other Indian groups that spoke the same language.

Since 1540, the Mohave people have overcome many challenges created by outsiders. Through years of difficult times, the Mohave people have survived and even prospered. Today, they continue to work hard to preserve their **heritage**.

CHAPTER TWO

VILLAGES AND HOMES

The desert and the Colorado River were the main features of the Mohave Indians' territory. It didn't rain much, and the land was extremely dry. The Colorado River was a valuable source of water, especially during the hot summer months when temperatures reached more than 105° Fahrenheit (40.5° C).

The Mohave lived in small settlements. The largest villages rarely had more than 50 people living in them. Villages were often moved and reorganized. Each person may have lived in several settlements during their lifetime.

Houses were made of logs and built in deep pits. The outside of each house was covered with mud and grass. The surrounding soil helped keep the structure cool during the fierce summer heat. Most houses had a fire pit in the center for cooking. A single door, which faced south, let sunlight in and allowed cooking smoke to escape.

Mohave homes had a rectangular floor plan. Three of the four sides sloped toward a flat roof made of thatch and reeds.

CHAPTER THREE

FROM FARMING TO FISHING

The Mohave Indians learned basic farming methods from other groups of American Indians who lived farther south in what is now northern Mexico. Their major food crops were corn, beans, and squash. They planted seeds in the rich black soil deposited along the riverbanks during summer floods. Crops grew quickly in the warm temperatures and were ready for harvest in the early fall.

Women and children gathered seeds, roots, and greens. Wild plants made up about half of the Mohave people's meals. Plants were also used as medicines and as materials for tools and crafts.

The Mohave hunted small animals such as rabbits, rats, mice, and birds. They also caught fish in the Colorado River. They used a combination of spears, nets, and basket traps to capture fish. The Mohave also fished along the riverbanks using boats made from reeds.

Few large animals lived in Mohave territory. To hunt larger animals, such as bighorn sheep, deer, and pronghorn antelope, Mohave men sometimes traveled into the territories of neighboring groups.

PRONGHORN
ANTELOPE

CHAPTER FOUR

COOKING MEALS

Mohave women were usually in charge of preparing meals for their family. Many of their dishes were similar to modern stews or porridges.

The Mohave cooked many foods over an open flame. Meals were sometimes baked in earth or sand ovens or roasting pits. Meat or vegetables were wrapped in leaves or reeds before being cooked. After a few hours in the hot pit, the food would be ready to eat.

Mohave cooks also built fires to smoke meat and fish. The flesh would be cut into long, narrow strips and placed on a rack or a low branch over the flame. Smoked meat and fish could be stored for later use. Corn, seeds, and many types of wild plants were ground into powder using stone tools called metates, manos, pestles, and mortars.

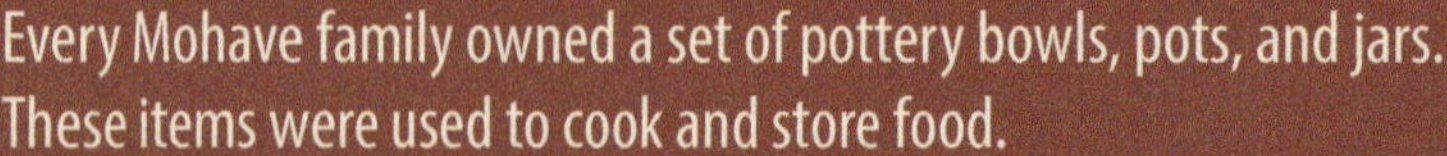

Every Mohave family owned a set of pottery bowls, pots, and jars. These items were used to cook and store food.

CHAPTER FIVE

CRAFTING WITH NATURE

The Mohave people used items found in their **environment** to create many kinds of tools and beautiful objects for everyday use. Mohave women made baskets, fish traps, drums, and trays out of woven plant fibers. Some clothing was made from plant fibers, too. Plants were also used in religious **rituals** or to make powerful medicines.

The Mohave people used wood to make items such as arrows, bows, spears, and war clubs. Reeds were used to build rafts that could hold up to five people.

Mohave men chipped pieces of stone to make sharp tools such as knives, spearheads, and arrowheads. They made other useful tools by grinding rocks together. Two commonly used types of stone were basalt and sandstone.

Animals provided more than food for the Mohave people. Skins and furs were turned into bags, ropes, blankets, and clothing. Animal bone was used to make game pieces, hairpins, and needles.

Mohave craftspeople used clay from nearby rivers to make jars, bowls, pots, trays, dishes, and toys, such as this doll. Some types of pottery were painted with red decorations.

CHAPTER SIX

MOHAVE SOCIAL STRUCTURE

The smallest Mohave social unit was the family. The oldest male was responsible for leading this group. Some men were allowed to have more than one wife. Mohave men and women could remarry many times. Each Mohave family had its own land for farming and gathering. Other people weren't allowed to use these resources unless the family that owned them said it was okay.

Some Mohave men owned female slaves who had to take orders from the family members. Except for these slaves, most Mohave considered themselves equal. A man was given special recognition if he was generous or if he defeated many enemies in battle.

Mohave families were joined together to form 22 clans. The members of each group claimed to have a common **ancestor**, such as the sun or a rattlesnake. Individuals had to marry people outside their clan.

The Mohave had a **complex** social structure. An individual's status depended on if they were a man or a woman, and their age, wealth, and family connections.

CHAPTER SEVEN

GOVERNMENT AND WARFARE

The Mohave people were ruled through a system of political leaders who had different amounts of power. Each village had a chief, but none of the chiefs had absolute power over the people. The villages were combined to form three large districts, which were each ruled by a leader called a super chief. The super chief with the highest **status** made important decisions for the Mohave people.

Chiefs and super chiefs were the most honored people in Mohave society. They were given many gifts by their followers. The position of chief was usually handed down from father to son. Some leaders were chosen by the community based on their knowledge and abilities.

The Mohave people fought together under the control of the senior super chief. They fought for many reasons, including to conquer lands or because they or their neighbors were capturing slaves or stealing food.

Early Mohave warriors often used bows, such as the one shown here, to shoot arrows during combat. They also fought using clubs and spears. They sometimes carried round leather shields for protection.

CHAPTER EIGHT

RELIGIOUS BELIEFS AND PRACTICES

Some Mohave people were healers or religious leaders. They often collected sacred objects and performed rituals that were supposed to give them special powers. These people were often feared because they could use their abilities for good or evil.

The Topock Maze in Needles, California, is believed to be an important Mohave spiritual site where good souls passed into the afterlife and bad souls became lost.

A group of Mohave Indians gathered in the early 1900s to **mourn** the death of their chief, Sistuma.

The Mohave people's religion taught them things they needed to know to be good members of their community. Many of their religious beliefs involved dreams. They believed that many supernatural forces communicated with them while they slept. Throughout people's lives, there were special occasions when their dreams gave them direction. The Mohave believed the most important dreams came when boys became men and girls became women.

Mohave children spent a great deal of time learning religious songs and rituals. These educational sessions included information about history and supernatural beings, as well as the deeds of famous warriors. Stories told by community elders helped young people understand their faith.

CHAPTER NINE

EUROPEANS IN THE SOUTHWEST

The Mohave people encountered Europeans for the first time in the mid-16th century. Around 1540, Hernando de Alarcón sailed up the Colorado River. This and other European explorations began a difficult period for American Indians in the Southwest.

During the next 200 years, Spanish treasure hunters, soldiers, and **missionaries** passed through the region. By the end of the 18th century, European colonists were living in what is today California and Arizona. Even so, the vast deserts that surrounded the river kept most newcomers away from Mohave territory.

The Europeans brought many changes to the Southwest. New diseases, such as measles and smallpox, spread quickly with terrifying results. Among some American Indian groups, as many as 90 percent of the people died. It's likely the Mohave also suffered terrible losses between 1550 and 1700.

Hernando de Alarcón was a Spanish explorer. He was one of the first Europeans to set foot in Alta California, or the present-day state of California.

After 1750, Spain began developing **missions** and military colonies close to the Colorado River. The Spanish created a route to connect their settlements in western California to those in Arizona and northern Mexico. The Spanish also set up two settlements to the south of the Mohave, among their close **allies**, the Quechan people. Less than a year later, the Mohave and the Quechan destroyed these settlements.

In 1775, a large group of colonists moved from Arizona to California. The newcomers' animals destroyed the Mohave and the Quechan people's crops in 1781, and the American Indians decided the colonists couldn't be trusted. Angered, the Mohave burned the missions and towns and killed or captured all of the Spanish colonists. Because of this, more Europeans arrived with a large army, and war continued for several years. In 1783, the Europeans left and the Quechan and Mohave people celebrated victory.

This illustration from the mid-19th century shows what life was like in Mohave territory around this time. European settlers were slowly moving into the area, forever changing how the Mohave Indians lived.

CHAPTER TEN

THE MEXICAN PERIOD

The Mexican period of California's history began in 1821, when Mexico became independent of Spain. In 1825, the government in Mexico City ordered troops to conquer the Quechan and the Mohave peoples. However, the armies were called back after a revolt broke out among the Yaquis of northwestern Mexico.

By 1850, the Mohave had driven away incoming Europeans from several directions. They were also successful in their wars against other native peoples. The Chemehuevi Indians helped the Mohave in battle. In return, the Chemehuevi people were given captured areas of land along the river to use for their villages. For many years, the Mohave were able to prevent outsiders from moving into their territory. By the time of the U.S.-Mexican War (1846–1848), the Mohave people had established themselves as a strong and fearsome group in western North America.

In 1871, Lieutenant George M. Wheeler set out to explore and map the land west of the 100th **meridian**. He brought along several Mohave Indians as guides.

CHAPTER ELEVEN

THE AMERICANS MOVE WEST

At the end of the U.S.-Mexican War, the U.S. government claimed the Mohave territory. The Mohave would soon face the U.S. Army, but they weren't afraid. They believed in their future as a conquering people.

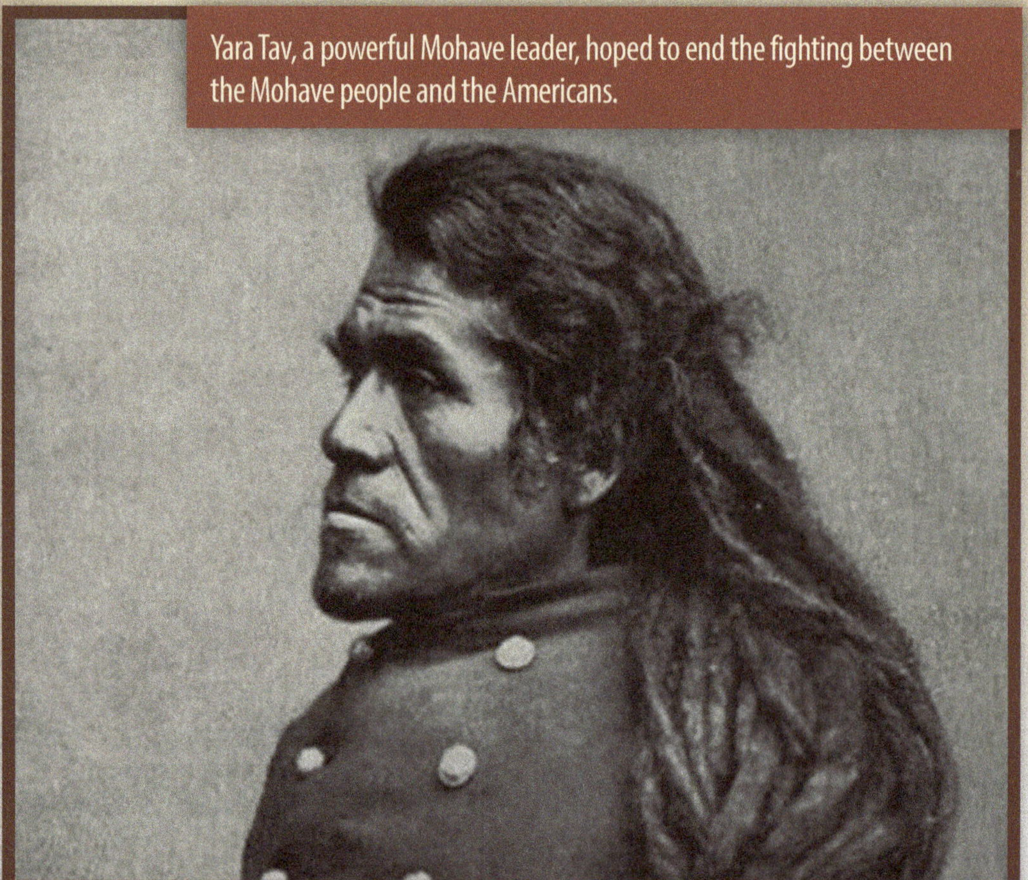

Yara Tav, a powerful Mohave leader, hoped to end the fighting between the Mohave people and the Americans.

By the mid-1850s, the Mohave territory had become a crossroads. In 1852, the Mohave saw the first steamboat to travel up the Colorado River. The people who used the north-south route of the river included Mormons who were headed for Utah. The gold rush also brought many travelers to the area.

Yara Tav wanted to find a peaceful solution to the problem. He visited the outsiders' cities of Los Angeles and San Francisco. He even met with President Abraham Lincoln on the East Coast. When Tav returned to his people, he argued for peace. He knew the Mohave would not find victory if they continued to fight the newcomers.

CHAPTER TWELVE

RESERVATION LIFE

In 1864, explorer Charles Poston held a conference with American Indian leaders to discuss the formation of a **reservation**. The Colorado River Reservation in Arizona opened in 1865, but many Mohave were against moving there. They felt the Americans usually lied to them. They didn't want to live in poor conditions and according to the rules of their enemies.

For the first time, the Mohave people were seriously divided. American Indians who refused to live on reservations were often killed without a trial. The U.S. Army continued its takeover, building new reservations and forcing the surviving American Indians onto them.

The fighting finally ended in 1890. However, life on the reservations remained very difficult for the American Indians. They faced **racism**, poverty, and **discrimination** every day. There were also food shortages and disease.

By 1910, there were around 1,000 Mohave people living on reservations in Arizona and California. Many had taken up European ways of life, including clothing styles, tools, and farming methods.

CHAPTER THIRTEEN

MODERN-DAY MOHAVE

Gradually, attitudes about American Indians began to change. Starting in 1930, many government policies even helped, rather than hurt, the Mohave communities. In 1937, the first modern tribal government was formed at the Colorado River Reservation.

In 1957, the Mohave created the Fort Mohave Constitution. The Fort Mojave community is ruled by a seven-member council. The reservation includes 33,000 acres (13,354.6 ha) of land and extends into California, Arizona, and Nevada. The Colorado River Indian Reservation is even larger and extends into California and Arizona.

Today, thousands of people of Mohave **descent** live along the Colorado River. Many reservations are becoming major tourist spots because of the fishing and boating opportunities the river provides. Mohave leaders are at the front of the struggle to preserve what remains of the Colorado River environment. The story of the Mohave Indians is an example of the ability of a proud people to survive and prosper, even after many challenging years of hardship.

GLOSSARY

ally (AA-ly) One of two or more people or groups who work together.

ancestor (AN-ses-tuhr) Someone in your family who lived long before you.

complex (kahm-PLEKS) Not easy to understand or explain; having many parts.

descent (dih-SENT) The background of a person in terms of their family or nationality.

discrimination (dis-krih-muh-NAY-shun) Different—usually unfair—treatment based on factors such as a person's race, age, religion, or gender.

environment (en-VY-urn-muhnt) The natural world around us.

heritage (HEHR-uh-tihj) The traditions and beliefs that are part of the history of a group or nation.

meridian (muh-RIH-dee-uhn) One of the lines that run north to south between the poles on maps of Earth.

mission (MIH-shun) A community established by a church for the purpose of spreading its faith.

missionary (MIH-shuh-nehr-ee) Someone who travels to a new place to spread their faith.

mourn (MORN) To show or feel sadness.

racism (RAY-sih-zum) The belief that one group or race of people is better than another group or race.

reservation (reh-zuhr-VAY-shun) Land set aside by the government for specific American Indian nations to live on.

ritual (RIH-choo-uhl) A religious ceremony, especially one consisting of a series of actions performed in a certain order.

status (STAA-tuhs) Position or rank in relation to others.

INDEX

PRIMARY SOURCE LIST

Page 7
Two Mohave Indian girls standing in front of a dwelling with a thatched roof. Photograph. Charles C. Pierce. 1900. Now kept in the California Historical Society Collection, San Francisco, CA.

Page 17
Maiman, a Mohave Indian. Photograph. Timothy H. O'Sullivan. 1871. Now kept at the Library of Congress Prints and Photographs Division, Washington, D.C.

Page 19
Mohave Indians mourning over the body of their dead chief, Sistuma. Photograph. Charles C. Pierce. ca. 1902. Now kept in the California Historical Society Collection, San Francisco, CA.

WEBSITES

Due to the changing nature of Internet links, PowerKids Press has developed an online list of websites related to the subject of this book. This site is updated regularly. Please use this link to access the list: www.powerkidslinks.com/saic/moh